My first tunnel!

Me and Spider

The family vacation—
on Compost Island

JUN 08

For "the boys"—
Ken, Sean, Ryan, Patrick and Timothy
—D.C.

For Rozzie and Cheetah
—H.B.

Diary of a Worm Text copyright © 2003 by Doreen Cronin Illustrations copyright © 2003 by Harry Bliss
Printed in the U.S.A. All rights reserved. www.harperchildrens.com Library of Congress Cataloging-in-
Publication Data Cronin, Doreen. Diary of a worm / by Doreen Cronin ; pictures by Harry Bliss. p.   cm.
Summary: A young worm discovers, day by day, that there are some very good and some not so good things
about being a worm in this great big world. ISBN 0-06-000150-X – ISBN 0-06-000151-8 (lib. bdg.)
[1. Worms–Fiction.   2. Diaries–Fiction.]   I. Bliss, Harry, 1964– ill.   II. Title. PZ7.C88135 Di   2003
[E]–dc21 2002007949 Typography by Alicia Mikles 21 22 23 24 25 26 27 28 29 30 ❖ First Edition

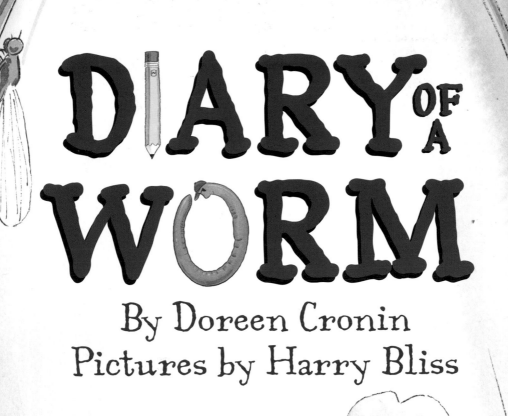

DIARY OF A WORM

By Doreen Cronin
Pictures by Harry Bliss

JOANNA COTLER BOOKS

An Imprint of HarperCollins Publishers

MARCH 20

Mom says there are three things I should always remember:

1. The earth gives us everything we need.

2. When we dig tunnels, we help take care of the earth.

3. Never bother Daddy when he's eating the newspaper.

First all of his legs got stuck.

Then he swallowed a bunch of dirt.

Tomorrow he's going to teach
me how to walk upside down.

MARCH 30
Worms cannot walk upside down.

APRIL 4

Fishing season started today.
We all dug deeper.

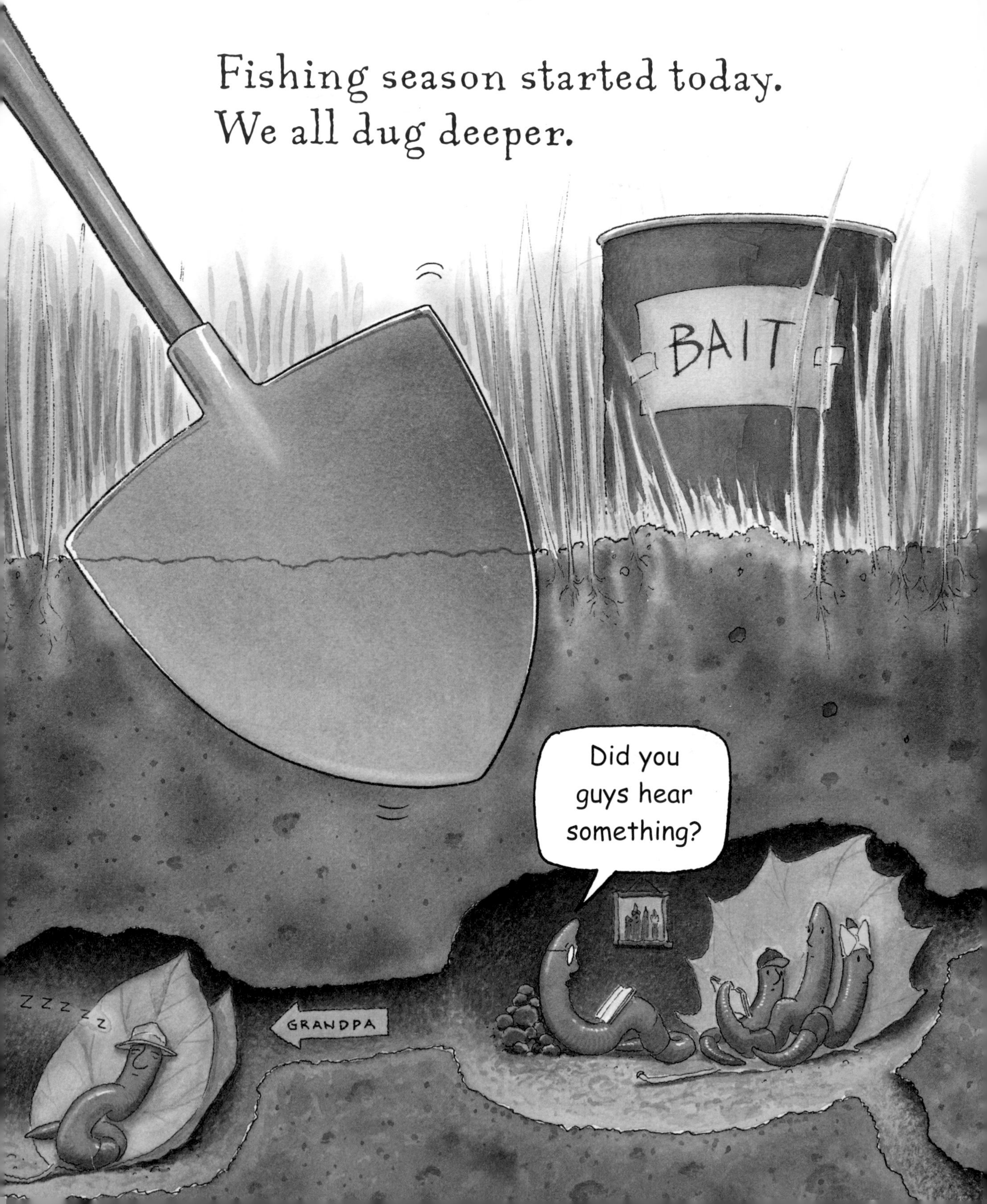

APRIL 10

It rained all night and the ground was soaked. We spent the entire day on the sidewalk.

Hopscotch is a very dangerous game.

APRIL 15

I forgot my lunch today.
I got so hungry that I ate
my homework.

My teacher made me write "I will not eat my homework" ten times.

When I was finished, I ate that, too.

APRIL 20

I snuck up on some kids in the park today. They didn't hear me coming.

I wiggled up right between them and they SCREAMED.

I love when they do that.

MAY 1

Grandpa taught us that good manners are very important.

So today I said "good morning" to the first ant I saw.

MAY 8

Had the worst nightmare
last night—

giant birds playing hopscotch.

Mom says I have to stop eating so much garbage right before I go to bed.

MAY 15

I got into a fight with Spider today.
He told me you need legs to be cool.
Then he ran. I couldn't keep up.
Maybe he's right.

MAY 16

I made Spider laugh so hard,
he fell out of his tree.
Who needs legs?

MAY 28

Last night I went to the school dance.

You put your head in.

You put your head out.

You do the hokey pokey and
you turn yourself about.

That's all we could do.

I brought mine home and
we ate it for dinner.

JUNE 15

My older sister thinks she's so pretty. I told her that no matter how much time she spends looking in the mirror, her face will always look just like her rear end.

Spider thought that
was really funny.

Mom did not.

JULY 4

When I grow up, I want to be a Secret Service agent. Spider says I will have to be very careful because the president might step on me by mistake.

Three things I don't like
about being a worm:

1. I can't chew gum.

2. I can't have a dog.

3. All that homework.

Three good things about being a worm:

1. I never have to go to the dentist.

2. I never get in trouble for tracking mud through the house.

3. I never have to take a bath.

AUGUST 1

It's not always easy being a worm. We're very small, and sometimes people forget that we're even here.

But, like Mom always says, the earth never forgets we're here.

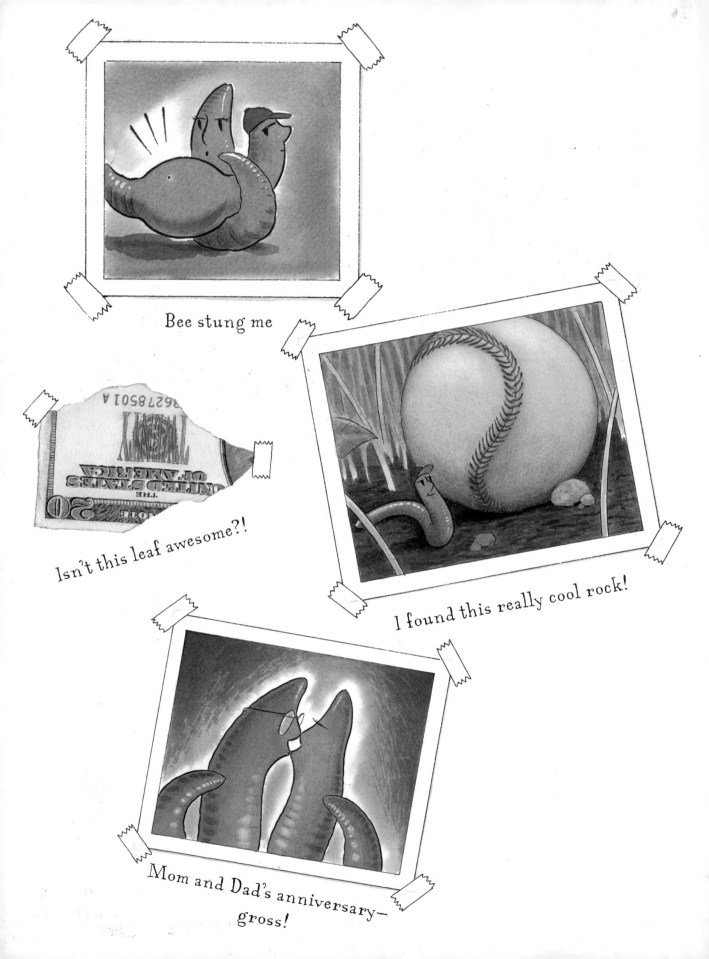

Bee stung me

Isn't this leaf awesome?!

I found this really cool rock!

Mom and Dad's anniversary—
gross!